To: Cora and Dorothy

From: Ashlie, Will and

ELLOOTT

Emmy Mermaid and the Fantastic Seahorse Race

Bright Sparks ☆

It was a normal day in the Enchanted City. Mermaids and mermen went about their business as usual. Suddenly there was a distant **RUMBLING**, and within seconds a whirlwind had hit the streets! The water swirled in every direction - hats went flying and one little mermaid lost her balance completely and fell on her bottom.

A great cry of **"YAHOoooooooooooo!"** rose and then vanished into the distance as the disturbance passed. "It's that *Emmy* racing her seahorses again!" cried the old couple, shaking their fists after her.

The King's messenger finally caught up with Emmy and summoned her to the King.

"Now Emmy, I will not have this **YAHOOING** through my streets!" he said sternly. "I've racked my brains for the perfect punishment and I am putting YOU in charge of the celebrations for Enchanted City Day!"

Then he smiled to himself and thought, "That should keep her quiet for a while!"

Emmy went to complain to Pearl the Curl.

"Enchanted City Day is the most important holiday of our year!" she wailed. "What am I going to do?"

"Let's think," said Pearl. "What was the King punishing you for?"

"Riding my seahorses too fast in the street," grumbled Emmy.

"That's it!" cried Pearl. "You should hold a race!"

Soon everyone was talking about the Great Seahorse Race.

"I bet I win," cried Gary Glory. "I'm really **FAST**."

"You haven't even got a seahorse to ride," said Buster Blowfish sensibly.

"Well I'll borrow one. Emmy's got lots."

"I never learned to ride," said Vinnie Tuna in his usual gloomy way. "I'm sure I'd fall off."
"You can't fall off," explained Buster patiently. "You're a fish - you'd just float off."

Everyone was going around saying, "I bet I win!" or, " I bet Emmy wins!" and soon Gary had an idea.

"Since everyone's **SO** eager to bet," he announced, "I'm going to make it official.
Step right up and place your bets! Only one seashell to place a bet."

"Young man!" said Oscar Octopus, swimming up behind Gary, who was struggling with a large bag of seashells. "What do you intend to do with all your earnings?"
Gary looked astonished. "I'm going to buy myself lots of **FANTASTIC** stuff, of course," he said.

"Oh no, you're not!" said Oscar. "You know the rules. Betting is only allowed if it's for fun or for charity. You can give those seashells to the school in the Enchanted City."

"Do I have to?" grumbled Gary. But he did as he was told.

The day of the Great Seahorse Race arrived. Everyone flooded to the
Enchanted City Racetrack. The contestants were all feeling very **NERVOUS**.
"I really don't think I should be doing this," trembled Vinnie Tuna, looking very pale.
Buster secretly felt the same way, but he said, "Don't be silly, it's just for fun."
"I'm going to win!" cried Gary.

Just then Emmy came storming up to the starting post on a beautiful, sleek horse. Her saddle and bridle were made of silk, and she wore a peaked jockey cap.

"Everyone ready?" she called cheerfully.

The King dropped the flag and the riders were off! Gary made a tremendous start, but then he seemed to lose his balance, and soon he was swimming furiously after his horse. Buster was running a good race.

Scuttle the Crab was clinging furiously to the back of a very old, tired seahorse that didn't want to be in the race anyway. Sizzle and Slink, the electric eels, shared a horse and seemed to be doing pretty well. Pearl rode side-saddle and looked very pretty, waving to all the spectators.

But Emmy! Emmy rode like the wind.

The water swirled and whirled around her, and no one had any chance of keeping up.

She wasn't even riding the best horse in her stable - she had lent that to Gary Glory -

but she was such a good rider that it didn't make a bit of difference.

She whistled past the finishing line, the flag came down, and a cheer went up.

"Hurrah for Emmy! The **FASTEST** mermaid in town!"

"Well Emmy," said the King with a smile.

"It's nice to give you a medal for riding too fast instead of a punishment!"

"Thank you, Your Majesty!" said Emmy.

Then she turned to the crowds. "Food is being served in the pink striped tent!" she announced. Howie waved from the tent where he had been busy all day making a pot of seaweed surprise. "And there are lots of other races!" cried Emmy.

When everyone had had enough to eat and drink, the fun races began. There was an egg-and-spoon race which Vinnie Tuna won, much to his astonishment.

"But I never win anything!" he protested,

looking quite overcome with emotion as the King gave him his medal.

Next there was a sack race. Pearl the Curl almost won this race, but at the last minute she tripped on her curly fins, and Gary Glory beat her to the finish line.

"Hurrah for me!" cried Gary. Then he caught sight of Pearl's face. "We'll share the prize,"
he said promptly. "You would have won if it wasn't for your fins."
"Well done, my boy!" beamed Oscar Octopus.

Afterward there was a cartwheeling race. The King roared with laughter as he watched the fish trying to spin on their fins. No one was any good at it except for Oscar Octopus, who could turn **SPECTACULAR** cartwheels.

Thanks to his eight arms he covered more ground in a single cartwheel than anyone, so
he won the race and was sitting enjoying a glass of seaweed surprise, keeping score,
and signing autographs by the time the first runner-up arrived at the finish line.

In the evening, when everyone started to get tired,
there were jugglers and plate-spinners and mermaids walking on stilts.
There was a clownfish, and a crab that made **FANTASTIC** animals out of balloons.

Scuttle was very impressed, but afterward, when he tried to make one himself,
his sharp claws kept bursting the balloons.

Finally there was a big parade. Everyone who had won prizes rode at the front, and Emmy had pride of place in the King's chariot.

"You've done very well, Emmy," said the King, patting her shoulder.
"I'm very proud of you. In the future, perhaps you'll put your energy into
organizing fantastic things like this, instead of wasting it by yahooing through my streets!"
Emmy grinned back at him, but she made no promises!

This is a Bright Sparks Book
First published in 2000

Bright Sparks
Queen Street House
4 Queen Street
Bath BA1 1HE, UK

This book was created by
small world creations ltd
Tetbury,UK

Written by Janet Allison Brown
Illustrated by Matt Ward
Designed by Sarah Lever

© Parragon 2000

Printed in Spain

ISBN 1 - 84250 - 033 - 3